Bea Rocks the Flock

THE FLOCK

Victoria Jamieson

BLOOMSBURY

NEW YORK BERLIN LONDON

Bea wanted to be a good sheep. But she had a hard time following the Rule of Sheepdom:

SHEEP ARE NOT UNIQUE!

Flossie fretted when Bea showed her true colors.

Mossie got miffed when Bea danced to the beat of her own drum.

And Jean was just plain bossy when Bea broke the rules!

With a sniff and a snort, Bea packed her backpack and said farewell to the flock.

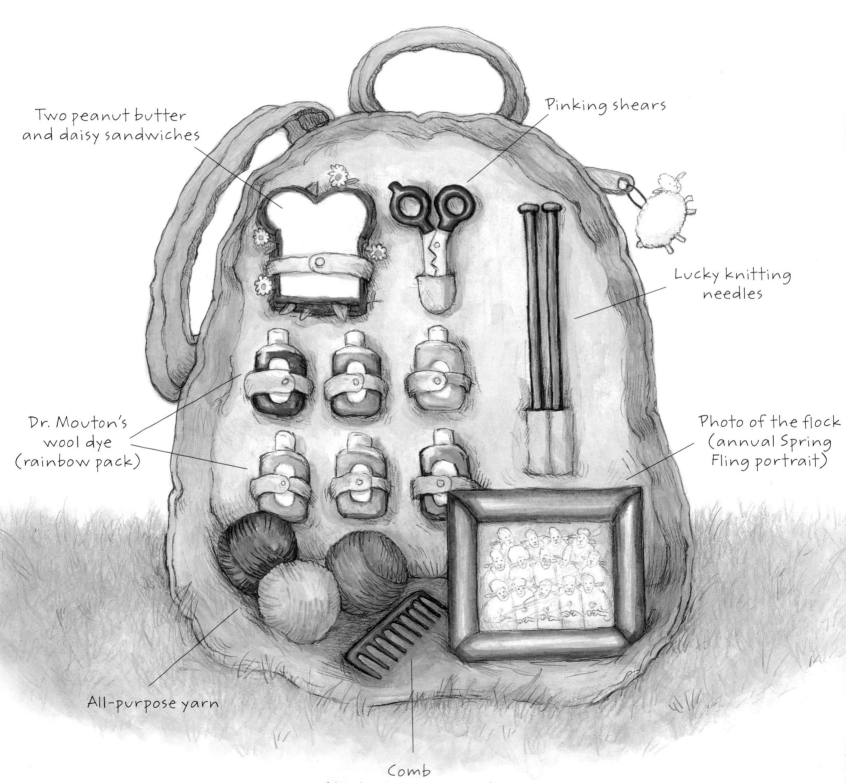

Two peanut butter and daisy sandwiches

Pinking shears

Lucky knitting needles

Dr. Mouton's wool dye (rainbow pack)

Photo of the flock (annual Spring Fling portrait)

All-purpose yarn

Comb (for bad-fleece days)

"I will miss you all terribly," called Bea. "But since I am not appreciated here, I will start a new life for myself in the big city."

"Great clanging cowbells!" shouted Bea as she zoomed down the city street. Everyone looked different, and no one was doing anything the same way.

"This is where I belong!"

First, Bea did some sightseeing.

But she couldn't be a tourist forever. If she wasn't going to be a sheep anymore, then what could she be?

"Aha! I've got it!"
She pulled out some yarn and got to work. By morning she was ready to start her no-rules-following, free-as-can-be life.

Sheep Meadow

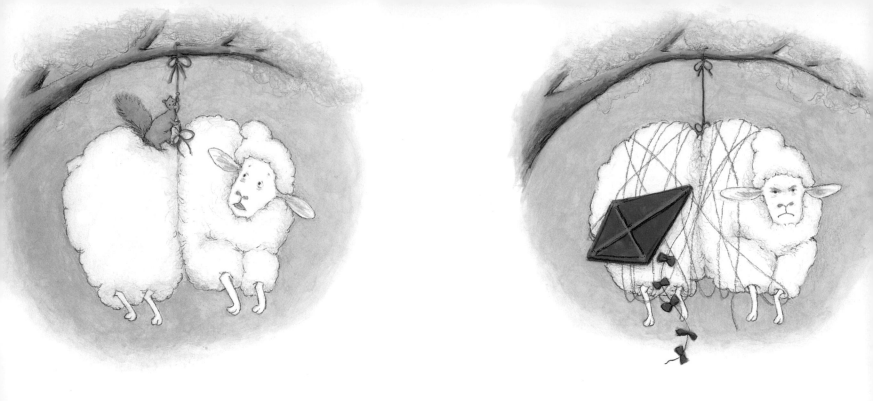

But Bea's new life was not as carefree as she had expected.

She needed a new plan. Hanging around in the sky was boring. Where was the most interesting place in the whole city?

"Eureka! I've got it!" Bea snatched the pinking shears and comb from her backpack and got to work. By morning she was ready to start her new, chock-full-of-stories, interesting life.

But her new interesting life was a little *too* interesting.

Even the most interesting places were lonely without friends.

"What I need is a new flock of glamorous city friends."

"Gadzooks! I've got it!"
She yanked the pink dye out of her backpack and got to work. By morning she was ready to start life with a new flock of big-city friends.

SHEEPDOG COMPETITION

But her big-city friends turned out to be big pains in the neck!

Her friends on the farm may have been fussy, picky, and bossy, but Bea missed them.

"Oh, what should I do?"

"Pardon me," called the judge. "The results are in. You have been voted Most Unique Dog . . .

. . . I mean, Sheep!"

Bea could not believe her ears. If she could be a sheep *and* be unique, then maybe the Rule of Sheepdom was wrong.

"Good-bye, big city!" she called. "You are interesting and fun and exciting . . . but so am I. And I'm not afraid to show it anymore!"

Nothing in the big city made Bea as happy as seeing her flock again.

"It was so quiet when you were gone!" said Flossie.

"Things were boring here without you!" said Mossie.

Even Jean had to admit she was happy Bea was home. "You certainly are one of a kind," Jean grumbled. "But I guess you're one of OUR kind, because our flock is not a family without you!"

"That makes us a big one-of-a-kind family!" said Bea.
"Isn't there something unique that you've always wanted
to be?"

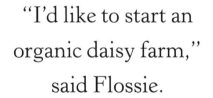

"I'd like to start an organic daisy farm," said Flossie.

"I've always wanted to open a painting school," said Mossie.

"You mean I can finally become a country western singer?" shouted Jean. "Being one of a kind is faaaaaaaaaaaabulous!"

Together, the flock voted on a new Rule of Sheepdom:

BEEEEEEEEEEEE yourself!

For Mom et Papa,

thank you for always encouraging me to be myself.

Published by Bloomsbury U.S.A. Children's Books
175 Fifth Avenue, New York, New York 10010

Library of Congress Cataloging-in-Publication Data
Jamieson, Victoria.
Bea rocks the flock / Victoria Jamieson. — 1st U.S. ed.
p.   cm.
Summary: Tired of being criticized for not being a good sheep, Bea decides to leave the flock and start a new life in the big city,
where she is certain that she will be more appreciated.
ISBN-13: 978-1-59990-260-9 • ISBN-10: 1-59990-260-5 (hardcover)
ISBN-13: 978-1-59990-357-6 • ISBN-10: 1-59990-357-1 (reinforced)
[1. Sheep—Fiction. 2. Individuality—Fiction. 3. City and town life—Fiction.] I. Title.
PZ7.J1568Be 2009   [E]—dc22   2008039175

Art created with acrylic paint
Typeset in Horley Old Style
Book design by Nicole Gastonguay

First U.S. Edition 2009
Printed in China
2 4 6 8 10 9 7 5 3 1 (hardcover)
2 4 6 8 10 9 7 5 3 1 (reinforced)

All papers used by Bloomsbury U.S.A. are natural, recyclable products made from wood grown in well-managed forests.
The manufacturing processes conform to the environmental regulations of the country of origin.